The Berenstain Bears®
MERRY CHRISTMAS

Stan & Jan Berenstain

Random House New York

The stories in this collection were originally published separately in the United States by
Random House Children's Books as the following:

The Berenstain Bears' Mad, Mad, Mad Toy Craze
copyright © 1999 by Berenstain Enterprises, Inc.

The Berenstain Bears Meet Santa Bear
copyright © 1984 by Berenstain Enterprises, Inc.

Random House and the colophon are registered trademarks of Penguin Random House LLC.

Visit us on the Web!
rhcbooks.com
BerenstainBears.com

Educators and librarians, for a variety of teaching tools,
visit us at RHTeachersLibrarians.com

ISBN 978-1-9848-9431-1

Printed in the United States of America
10 9 8 7 6

Contents

The Berenstain Bears'
MAD, MAD, MAD
TOY CRAZE

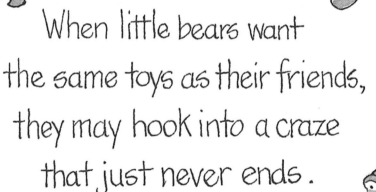

When little bears want
the same toys as their friends,
they may hook into a craze
that just never ends.

It was a calm and peaceful
afternoon in Bear Country. It
was calm and peaceful outside
the Bear family's tree house,
where the tulips were blooming
and the grass was growing.

It was calm and peaceful inside the tree house, where Papa Bear was reading the afternoon paper and Mama Bear was checking out the TV schedule.

But it was all over for peace and calm when
Brother and Sister came tearing home. They rushed
up the front steps and burst into the living room all
excited and so out of breath they could hardly talk.

"Papa . . . Mama," they gasped. "We need it . . . we gotta have it . . . we absolutely gotta—"

"Now, hold everything," said Papa. "Just calm down and tell me what it is that you need and absolutely gotta have."

"An advance!" sputtered Brother.

"That's right," gasped Sister. "An advance on our allowance. And if we don't get it, Herb's Hobby Shop is gonna run out!"

"Going to run out of what?" asked Papa.

"Why, Beary Bubbies, of course!" said Sister.

"And what, may I ask, are Boony Bearies, Booby Bubbies—whatever that was you said?" asked Papa.

"Beary Bubbies, Papa," said Brother. "They're terrific! They're great! They're fabulous!"

"And they're cute and adorable!" said Sister. "And each one is different and each one has its own name."

"Cousin Fred already has six of 'em!" said Brother.

"Lizzy has eight and Queenie has ten!" said Sister.

"Well," said Papa, reaching for his wallet and taking out some money, "far be it from me to deprive my cubs of Booby Bearies."

The money and the cubs disappeared so fast you'd have thought it was a magic act. "Well," said a bewildered Papa, "what do you suppose *that* was about?"

"Come to think of it," said Mama, "I did see a sign on Herb's Hobby Shop's window. It said 'We have Beary Bubbies!' I didn't think much about it. But I suppose that's what the cubs are talking about."

"*Talking about* is putting it mildly," said Papa. "They were flipping out about it. They were through the roof about it." He sighed. "It's just amazing to me," he said as he went back to his paper, "how otherwise sensible cubs can get pulled into any silly thing that comes along."

"I suppose," said Mama as she went back to the TV schedule.

The cubs ran all the way to Herb's Hobby Shop,

holding their precious Beary Bubby money

in their hot little hands.

HERB'S HOBBY SHOP

WE HAVE
BEARY
BUBBIES!
$2.95

And lucky cubs that they were, they got there in time to buy the last three Beary Bubbies in the store. "When do you expect more?" asked Brother.

"I can't say," said Herb. "I can't even get them on the phone. It's busy twenty-four hours a day."

Though it was true that Cousin Fred had six, Lizzy had eight, and Queenie had ten Beary Bubbies, while Brother and Sister had only three, the ones they had were really cute. Each one was different from the other and each one had its very own name.

Back home, Sister said, "We'd like to introduce our Beary Bubbies. This one is named Ziggy Zippo, this one is named Dimple Darling—"

"And this one is named Hairy Harry," said Brother.

"Hmm," said Papa as they all sat down to dinner.

"They *are* kind of cute," said Mama.

The next day, the cubs came to Papa with a proposition. "We won't ask for any more advances on our allowance if you'll hire us to do chores," said Brother.

"What are you going to do with the money you earn?" asked Papa.

"Buy more Beary Bubbies, of course," said Sister.

"But you said Herb's Hobby Shop is out of them and can't get more," said Papa.

"That's right," said Brother. "But Lizzy has two of a kind and she's willing to sell one for $5.00."

"So does Queenie," said Sister. "Only she wants $7.00."

"Hey," said Papa. "I thought they were just $2.95 at Herb's Hobby Shop."

"That's right," said Sister. "Only Herb's all out."

"Hmm," said Papa. "Buying and selling Beary Bubbies is beginning to sound like a pretty good business."

"Speaking of business," said Mama, "here's a piece in the paper about a fellow who bought a whole bunch of Beary Bubbies before they became popular. It says here that he just sold his entire collection for a fortune."

"Lemme see that!" said Papa, snatching the paper.
"Papa," said Brother. "About those chores?"

For the next couple of days,
Brother and Sister pulled weeds,

sorted trash,

and cleaned out cobwebs like there was no tomorrow.

Of course, there *were* more tomorrows— lots of them. And Brother and Sister were determined to spend them figuring out ways to get more Beary Bubbies.

"Just listen to this," said Papa, reading from a *Beary Bubbies* magazine he had found at the supermarket. "A rare Beary Bubby was sold in Bearville for hundreds of dollars! Did you hear that? Hundreds of dollars!"

That's when Brother and Sister burst in with the Beary Bubbies they had bought with their chore money. "Papa!" cried Brother. "We heard a rumor that the **TOYS IZ US** store in Big Bear City just got a shipment of Beary Bubbies!"

"A *huge* shipment!" cried Sister.

"Jump in the car!" cried Papa.

"But Big Bear City is twenty miles away," said Mama, following them out the door.

By the time Mama finished her sentence, Papa and the cubs were off in a cloud of dust.

"Look! A skywriter!" cried Sister as they roared along the road to Big Bear City.

"What does it say?" asked Papa.

"It says BEARY BUBBIES FOREVER!" said Brother.

"We'd better hurry," cried Papa, flooring the gas pedal, "or TOYS IZ US might run out!"

The rumor about TOYS IZ US turned out to be true. A huge banner said WE HAVE BEARY BUBBIES—$5! It looked like a big Beary Bubby party.

Only it was more like a big aggravation. The line wound around the store, babies were crying, and two daddies got into a shoving match about a place in line and had to be taken away by the police.

But the cubs got their Beary Bubbies. In fact, they headed home up to their necks in them.

Of course, not many things are forever—
and Beary Bubbies certainly weren't. Pretty
soon, Beary Bubbies were everywhere. They
came in Krinkly Krumbles cereal boxes.

You could get them at the
gas station with a fill-up.

You could get them with a Krazy Meal at the Burger Bear. After a while, just about everybody in Bear Country had so many Beary Bubbies that they didn't know what to do with them.

There wasn't much you *could* do with them in the first place. You couldn't play dolly with them the way you could with a good doll.

You couldn't play choo-choo with them the way you could with a toy train.

And no matter how many you had,
there was always somebody who had more.

The Berenstain Bears
MEET
SANTA BEAR

Special music's in the air
And Santa's at the mall.
What do the little bears
Make of it all?

It was just two days after Thanksgiving and the sights and sounds of Christmas could be seen and heard all over Bear Country.

"It seems to me," said Mama Bear as the Bear family arrived at the Bear Country Mall, "that the Christmas season starts earlier every year."

"Yes! Isn't it great?" said Papa Bear, admiring the mall decorations.

"I'm not so sure," sighed Mama. "I'm concerned about Brother and Sister Bear. Too much excitement isn't good for cubs."

"No need to be concerned," said Papa. "Brother and Sister are good little cubs. I'm sure they'll be calm and sensible about the whole thing."

But if Papa had looked at Brother and Sister at that moment, he wouldn't have been so sure. They were passing the big new toy store, and Brother and Sister didn't look the least bit calm and sensible.

They had just come from watching Saturday morning television and there had been lots of commercials for the new Christmas toys. Sister had wanted them all . . .

—a Bear-Hug Teddy, which hugged you back when you squeezed it; a ride-on pink pony; a clown-face mobile kit; and Giggly Goo, a strange substance that you could make into all sorts of funny shapes.

There had been some things that had
excited Brother, too . . .

—especially a remote-control robot
that could stand on its head, and a
dinosaur-molding kit.

TOY

And there they were, right in the toy store window—plus lots more! Sister was so excited, she was practically jumping up and down. And when Brother read a sign saying Santa Bear was coming to the mall to meet all his cub friends, she got even more excited.

COMING SOON
SANTA
BEAR
WILL BE HERE TO
MEET HIS FRIENDS

"Santa Bear!" she cried.
"Oh, Mama, may I come meet
Santa Bear? Please, may I?
Please?"

"In good time," said Mama,
sighing again. "Calm and
sensible, eh?" she said,
looking at Papa.

Sister Bear could hardly wait to start her Christmas list. She needed a little help from Brother with the hard words, but she didn't need any help thinking up things she wanted for Christmas!

DEAR SANTA BEAR,
This is my CHRISTMAS List:
BEAR-HUG TEDDY
HAPPY PINK PONY
Clown ~~MoBEEL~~ MOBILE
GIGGLY GOO
A RED BALL
BUBBLE PIPE
GUMBALL ~~MASHEEN~~ MACHINE
DOLLHOUSE FURNITURE
NEW D

Over the next few days the sights and sounds of Christmas became stronger and stronger and Sister's list grew longer and longer. After a while it looked like this—

(To see the rest of Sister's list, please turn the page.)

"You know," warned Brother, "if your list is too long, Santa Bear might think you're greedy and not bring you anything."

Sister hadn't thought of that!

"Santa Bear has a lot of cubs besides you to think about—all the cubs in the world."

She hadn't thought of that, either. As she looked at her long list she began to get a little nervous.

"Have you ever met Santa Bear?" she asked Brother.

"Sure," answered Brother, who was finishing up his list—which was very short. "A couple of years ago. He asked if I'd been good, then I told him what I wanted for Christmas and gave him my list, and that was that. It was fun."

Dear Santa Bear,
For Christmas I would like a robot that can stand on its head and a dinosaur-molding set and some surprises.
Thank you,
Brother Bear

Now Sister was really nervous. She thought of all the times she hadn't exactly been good. . . .

The time she and Brother had gotten into a fight and shouted at each other.

The time Mama's best lamp had gotten broken and they told a big lie.

And the time they had let their room get so messy that Mama had threatened to throw away all their toys.

"Oh, I wouldn't worry about those times," said Mama, giving Sister a little hug. "Santa Bear doesn't expect cubs to be perfect—just good." Then she said, "I hope you have your list ready, because tomorrow is the day you are going to meet Santa Bear."

Sister gulped. "It's *almost* ready," she said. "But what about *your* list for Santa—yours and Papa's?"

"Don't worry about that, sweetie," said Papa. "Santa Bear isn't for grown-ups. He's just for cubs."

"Pssst!" whispered Brother. "Presents for Mama and Papa is *our* job, silly! Come on, let's see how much you've got in your piggy bank."

Sister had just enough. Brother had enough and a little extra.

That evening Sister made a new list. It looked a lot like Brother's.

When they got to Santa Bear's little house in the mall the next day, there was a line. While Sister waited she began to think about Santa and what a hard job he had. She wondered how he took care of all those cubs; she wondered where he got all those presents; she wondered . . . then, before she could wonder another wonder, it was her turn and she was up on Santa Bear's big lap.

SEE SANTA BEAR ENTER HERE

"It's very nice to see you," he said in a deep, jolly voice. "Now, tell me, my dear, have you been good this year?"

"Well . . . ," said Sister, taking a deep breath, "I haven't been perfect, but I *have* been good." Then she told him what she wanted for Christmas and gave him her list.

Santa gave Sister and every other cub a souvenir coloring book. The cover showed him and his eight tiny reindeer flying through the starry night.

Sister's mind was so filled with thoughts about Santa that she almost forgot about the special shopping she had to do. But Brother remembered.

GIFT WRAP

TEA

They found just the right presents for Mama and Papa. Sister chose a fine new fur-brush for Papa and a lovely new pincushion for Mama. Brother bought Mama a box of her favorite breakfast tea and, for Papa, a handy pocket calculator.

"Look!" said Sister as they were leaving the mall. "Another Santa!" She was right. There, ringing a bell, was a rather skinny Santa with a scraggly beard. Beside him was a big iron pot that said HELP THE NEEDY.

"That's one of Santa's many helpers," explained Papa. "His job is to collect money to help the needy—birds who need seed, squirrels who didn't put enough aside for the winter."

The Bear family all put money in the pot. Sister had spent all hers and had to borrow some from Mama.

Finally the days and weeks of preparation and waiting were over and it was Christmas Eve.

"You know something, Papa?" said Sister as she helped hang the last holly wreath. "I've been thinking about Santa Bear and what a hard job he has. How can he visit every cub in the world in just a single night? Where does he get all those gifts? And besides— how can reindeer fly? And how can the sleigh land if it doesn't snow? And how can Santa come down our skinny little chimney?"

Papa took a deep breath, then looked up at the starry sky.

"I guess the answer, my dear, is that Christmas is such a special time that very special, almost magical things can happen. And the most magical thing of all is Santa Bear. I'd say he has the best job in the whole world, because the joy of giving is what Christmas is all about."

"I suppose," said Sister, "that Santa could just skip the chimney and come in the front door."

"I suppose," said Papa.

Then, before she went in, she took one last look at the starry sky. But it had clouded over. And now, instead of stars, there were snowflakes—thousands and thousands of small, silent snowflakes.

"Well," she thought. "At least that'll help with the sleigh."

When Sister woke up on Christmas morning, Bear Country was covered with a beautiful blanket of snow. And the floor beneath the Bears' Christmas tree was covered with piles of beautiful presents! What fun! What excitement! What shouting!

Then, when the excitement and shouting were over, the cubs watched Mama and Papa open *their* presents.

"What lovely, thoughtful gifts!" said Mama.

"Just what I wanted!" said Papa.

It was a very special moment. Sister knew right then and there that Papa was right: Santa Bear *did* have the best job in the whole world—because the joy of giving *was* what Christmas was all about.